This igloo book belongs to:

....

igloobooks

Published in 2017
by Igloo Books Ltd
Cottage Farm
Sywell
NN6 0BJ
www.igloobooks.com

LEO002 0517
2 4 6 8 10 9 7 5 3 1
ISBN 978-1-78670-288-3

Illustrated by Hilli Kushnir
Original story by Molly Wigand

Cover designed by Lee Italiano
Edited by Hannah Cather

Printed and manufactured in China

WAKE UP
SLEEPY
SLOTH

igloobooks

Sloth and I have been sleeping all day,
but it's time to start playing now.
Would you like to join us?

Wake up, Sleepy Sloth!

Hmm. That didn't work. We need to be louder. How loud can you say...

WAKE UP, SLEEPY SLOTH!

This sloth is fast asleep! What can we try next? Maybe we should shake the book.

Shake! Shake! Shake!

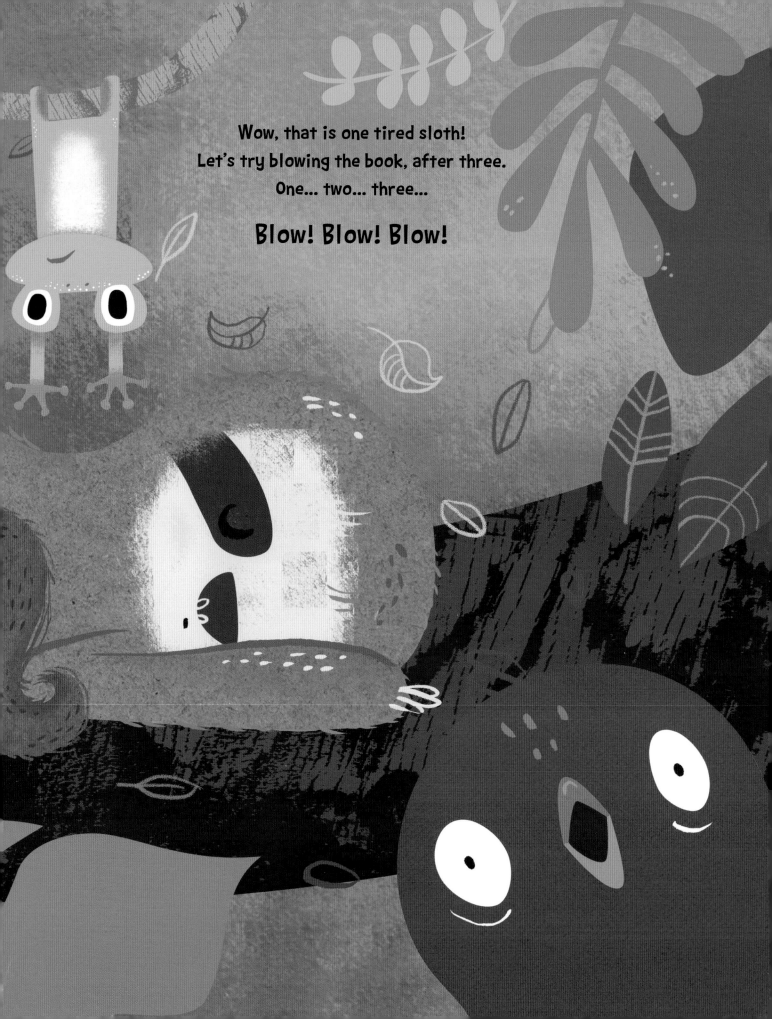

Wow, that is one tired sloth!
Let's try blowing the book, after three.
One... two... three...

Blow! Blow! Blow!

Talk about a lo-o-o-ong nap! This sloth is so sleepy.
How about if we twirl the book round and round?

Twirl! Twirl! Twirl!

Sorry, monkeys! We're just
trying to wake up the sloth,
but nothing is working.

What can we try next? I know.
Maybe Sloth will stop his snoozing if we
give the book a hug. Come on, get hugging!

Hug! Hug! Hug!

Well, that didn't work at all.
I'm running out of ideas!
Do you have any?

Brilliant! Yes, let's try tickling
the sloth. I'm sure that will do the trick.

Tickle! Tickle! Tickle!

Oh no! Even that didn't work.
We've tried shouting and shaking and blowing
and twirling and hugging and tickling...

There's one more thing we could try.
Perhaps if we ask nicely and say please,
Sleepy Sloth will surely wake up.

This is our last chance, so let's hope it works! Let's say it together. Ready?

PLEASE wake up, Sleepy Sloth.
PLEASE! PLEASE! PLEASE!

Hooray! Sloth has finally opened his eyes!
Hello, Sleepy Sloth! Thank you for waking up.

Now that Sloth is awake, who can we wake up next?
I know, that owl over there. Will you help me? Let's go!

Wake up, Sleepy Owl!